Dedications:

To my little monsters, may your magical spirits continue to soar.

– Love Mommy

Acknowledgments:

The authors are so grateful for the lifetime of holiday memories crafted so lovingly by their wonderful parents. Their devotion to family traditions serves as constant inspiration to hold the ones we love close and look for the magic in every day.

About the Authors:

This family has spent a lifetime loving Halloween in all its spooky splendor. Pumpkins and potions. Monsters and mischief. Cauldrons and cobwebs. All of it reminds them of countless years spent celebrating with over-the-top festivities and spirited fun. To them, Halloween is not just a holiday, it is a time for enchanted fun and magical moments with loved ones. Inspired by this philosophy, October Magic promises to bring the charming magic of All Hallows' Eve into your life no matter what the time of year.

This is a tale of the magic of Halloween, a cozy feeling so wonderful it's better than a dream...

It was a cool, crisp autumn eve and Harvest Moon glowed bright in the night sky.

Spotting a cheery, little pumpkin patch, Harvest Moon smiled and began to think about the magic of All Hallows' Eve.

Pictures of dark potions, bats, and ghostly ghouls, of round pumpkins, black cats, and witches brooms, circled around in its head.

And on this October night, Harvest Moon had a thought,
"I will start a brand new tradition right from this spot!"

Looking down upon the pumpkin patch, with its gourds big and small, Harvest Moon decided that it would find a special way to spread Halloween cheer.

While trick-or-treating and carving jack-o-lanterns was fun, Harvest Moon believed that more could be done to remind everyone how enchanting this time of year could be.

So, with a secret smile, it gathered all the magic it could and sprinkled it down onto the little pumpkin patch while chanting a silly spell:

Magic, mischief, and moonlight too!
Sprinkle, binkle, bankle boo!
Let's see what pumpkins can do!

PUMPKIN PATCH

The next day, when the pumpkin patch opened, there seemed to be a magical sparkle in the air. The corn mazes seemed taller, the hayrides seemed longer, and the carnival games prizes seemed grander.

Cheerful people oohed and ahhed at the rows and rows of pumpkins. Some were big and tall, others were short and squat. Some even had knobs, ridges, and spots!

Children picked out their perfect pumpkins, looking at them with wonder as they seemed to ooze magical mischief. A playful boy named Michael, with his little sister Jane, chose a plump, round one, perfect for carving.

When the day was at its end and they had to go home, they felt in their bones that this pumpkin would be memorable.

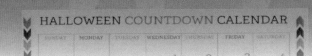

After getting home and putting their pumpkin on the table, the children climbed into bed with sleepy little smiles. That night they dreamed of sweet treats, silly costumes and sneaky pranks.

As the children slept, the magical pumpkin began to twinkle and shimmer. It rocked back and forth and began to shimmy and shake, to quiver and quake!

And then, when the moonlight hit the pumpkin just right, there was a loud "POP!"

And it burst with a flash of brilliant light!

The next morning, when the children came downstairs, they were amazed to find their pumpkin in broken pieces around the room. They decided to investigate and soon found a magical trail leading out of their room.

Following the trail, Michael and Jane looked high and low for what may have happened to their lovely little pumpkin.

Michael said "Maybe it was our cat that made the pumpkin go splat!" But Jane pointed to their sleeping cat and the magical trail which went right past him.

So they kept walking and to their shock, what did they see? A cozy punkin pixie, cute as can be.

Beside the punkin pixie sat a note. It read:

"Enchanted Greetings!

I'm a magic punkin sent to spread spooky cheer!
My new arrival to your house means just one thing,
You have finally reached the best time of the year!
What kind of surprises do you think I will bring?

You should know, I simply love to play trick or treat!
So, on some days a silly prank will be the way,
On others, I'll leave a treat that is ever so sweet.
And please know, I plot at night and sleep through the day!

Now that you know what I like to do,
I have left a fun surprise for you!"

Michael and Jane continued to follow the trail and stumbled upon a most magical scene.

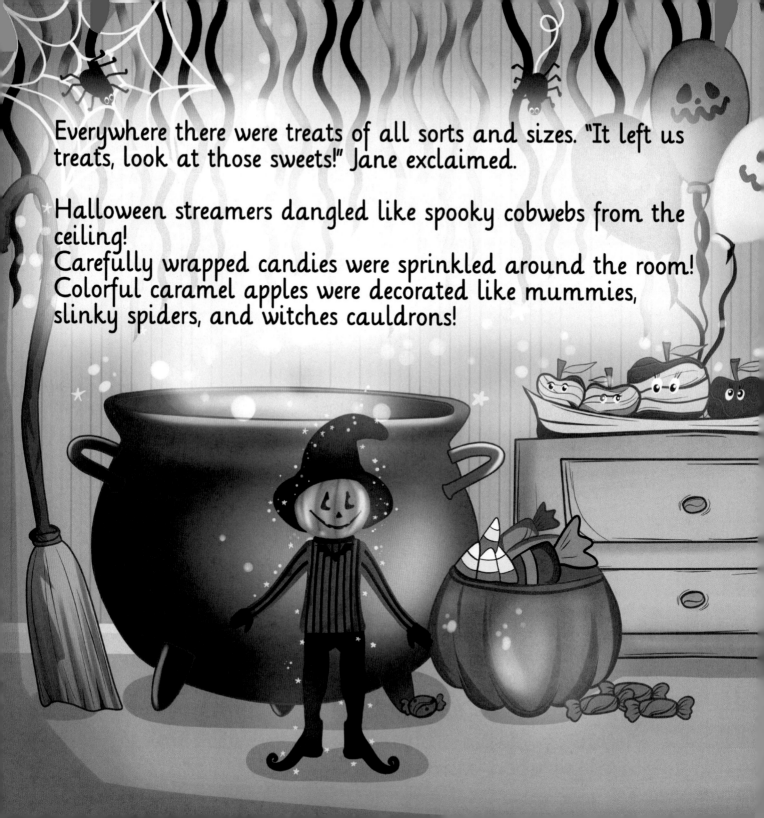

Everywhere there were treats of all sorts and sizes. "It left us treats, look at those sweets!" Jane exclaimed.

Halloween streamers dangled like spooky cobwebs from the ceiling!
Carefully wrapped candies were sprinkled around the room!
Colorful caramel apples were decorated like mummies, slinky spiders, and witches cauldrons!

The children's joyful eyes made it clear that the magic of Halloween was truly starting to spread. And as they went to bed that night, they wondered what kind of tricks the punkin pixie might play tomorrow.

Michael and Jane woke up hopeful that the punkin pixie had left them a prank to inspire different tricks they could play on Halloween night.

Looking around their bedroom, Michael and Jane were surprised to find spooky, spidery cobwebs swaying from the ceiling. Hopping out of bed, they ran to see what other shenanigans the punkin had gotten up to while they had slept.

The water in their toilets had turned colors like orange, purple, and black! Even their mother shrieked when she found big, round candy eyeballs in her ice cubes. That morning the laughter in their home did not stop as Halloween cheer continued to grow.

All over their little town, the children who had gotten a pumpkin from Harvest Moon's special pumpkin patch felt the spirit of Halloween spreading to everyone that they knew.

When people passed each other on the streets they no longer said, "Good morning!" or "Hello neighbor!" Instead, they greeted each other by saying "Happy Halloween!" or even "Ghostly Greetings!" On the playground, children talked about the crazy things their punkin pixies had gotten into the night before and the tasty treats it brought.

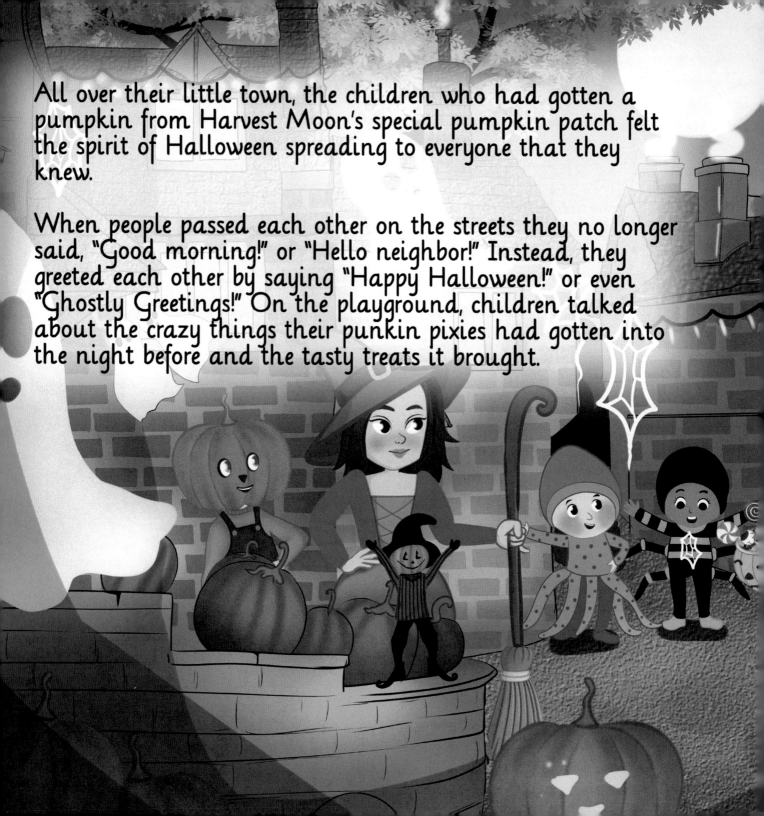

This was sure to be the best Halloween yet. And it was not because of the extra treats or the silly pranks, but because families and friends had been brought together by the special and powerful magic of All Hallows' Eve.

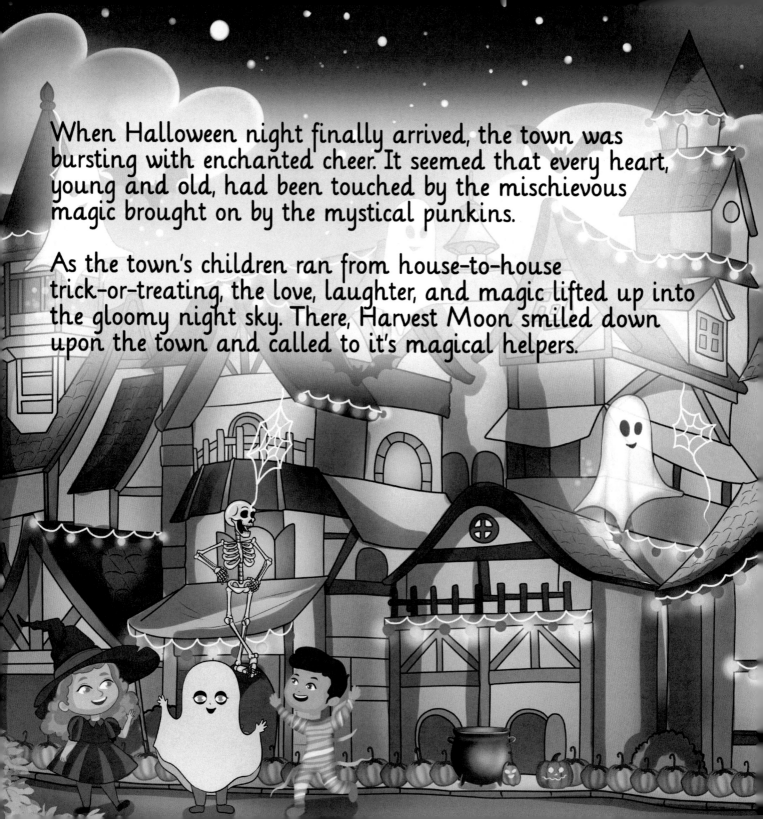

When Halloween night finally arrived, the town was bursting with enchanted cheer. It seemed that every heart, young and old, had been touched by the mischievous magic brought on by the mystical punkins.

As the town's children ran from house-to-house trick-or-treating, the love, laughter, and magic lifted up into the gloomy night sky. There, Harvest Moon smiled down upon the town and called to it's magical helpers.

It was time for the punkin pixies to go back to the pumpkin patch until next year when it was time for the spookiest season once again.

And as it walked back, the punkin pixie exclaimed: "Thanks for the laughs and all the Halloween fun, I can't wait until next year to see everyone!"

Every magical punkin pixie needs a name. What will yours be?

_____

When did the October magic start for you?

_____

Every punkin pixie is brought to life by chanting this spooky spell:

Magic, mischief, and moonlight too!
Sprinkle, binkle, bankle boo!
Let's see what pumpkins can do!

Made in the USA
Columbia, SC
18 October 2022

69266295R00015